Fifi's Frosty Morning

Created by Keith Chapman

This edition produced for The Book People Ltd,
Hall Wood Avenue, Haydock, St Helens WA11 9UL

First published in Great Britain by HarperCollins Children's Books in 2006

1 3 5 7 9 10 8 6 4 2
ISBN-13: 978-0-00-781398-8

Based on the television series *Fifi and the Flowertots* and the
original script 'Fifi's Frosty Morning' by Wayne Jackman
© Chapman Entertainment Limited 2006

Printed and bound in Hong Kong

Fifi's Frosty Morning

HarperCollins *Children's Books*

It was a very cold morning in Flowertot Garden. Fifi shivered in her bed as the doorbell rang. "Who can that be?" she said to herself, slipping into her slippers and going down the spiral staircase.

"**Brrr!** Hello Fifi," buzzed Bumble, tumbling through the door. "I've just been f...f...flying around and now I'm f...f...freezing!"

"Come in, Bumble," smiled Fifi, "let me get dressed and then I'll make us some ginger tea to warm us up."

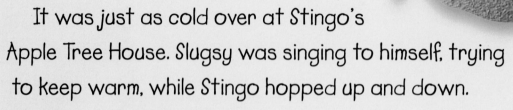

It was just as cold over at Stingo's
Apple Tree House. Slugsy was singing to himself, trying
to keep warm, while Stingo hopped up and down.
"Rotten Raspberries, I'm
frozen stiff!" Stingo said.
I wonder which Flowertot I
can trick, I mean charm, into
giving me a plate of hot
grub to warm me up?"
He peered through
his telescope at
Forget-Me-Not
Cottage.
But Fifi was having
problems of her
own...

Across the Garden, Pip and
Aunt Tulip were having great fun
with the frosty weather.
"Pip, look at these!"
Aunt Tulip called, pointing
out some beautiful icicles
hanging from a leaf.
"Oh, hello Pip and
Aunt Tulip," said Fifi
as she skipped
across the
Garden. "What
have you
found there?"
"Giant ice lollies!"
said Pip.

Fifi laughed,
"No, they're not
they're... oh,
Fiddly Flowerpetals, I've
forgotten!"

"Fifi Forget-Me-Not forgot!"

laughed Aunt Tulip. "They're icicles!"
Fifi gently struck them with a stick.
Each one made a beautiful sound.
"Can I have a go?" asked Pip.
"Of course," said Fifi, handing him the stick.
"I'm just on my way to Stingo's
anyway. Have fun!"

Slugsy was still singing
when Fifi arrived at
the Apple Tree House.
Stingo was very cold
and very miserable.
"Stingo?" called Fifi.
"Can you bring your tools
round and fix
my broken taps?"

"Bingo Stingo!"
grinned the naughty wasp.
"Well, I'm a bit busy right now –
unless you've got some
hot grub to feed me."
Stingo yelled down to Fifi.

"How about hot honey toast?" she offered.

"Sting-a-ling, I'm coming!" Stingo replied.

"Don't you want to hear my sssong, bosss?" asked Slugsy, sadly.

"In a word – No way!" called Stingo, already on the ground with his tools. Slugsy counted on his fingers and looked confused. "That's two words!" he sighed.

Soon, Stingo was stuffing himself with hot honey toast without giving the frozen pipes a second look. "Have you mended the pipes yet, Stingo?" Bumble asked nervously. "Nearly, a bit more honey toast should do it," Stingo muttered between mouthfuls. "The problem is the

ooja-ma-flip,

thingy-me-bob..."

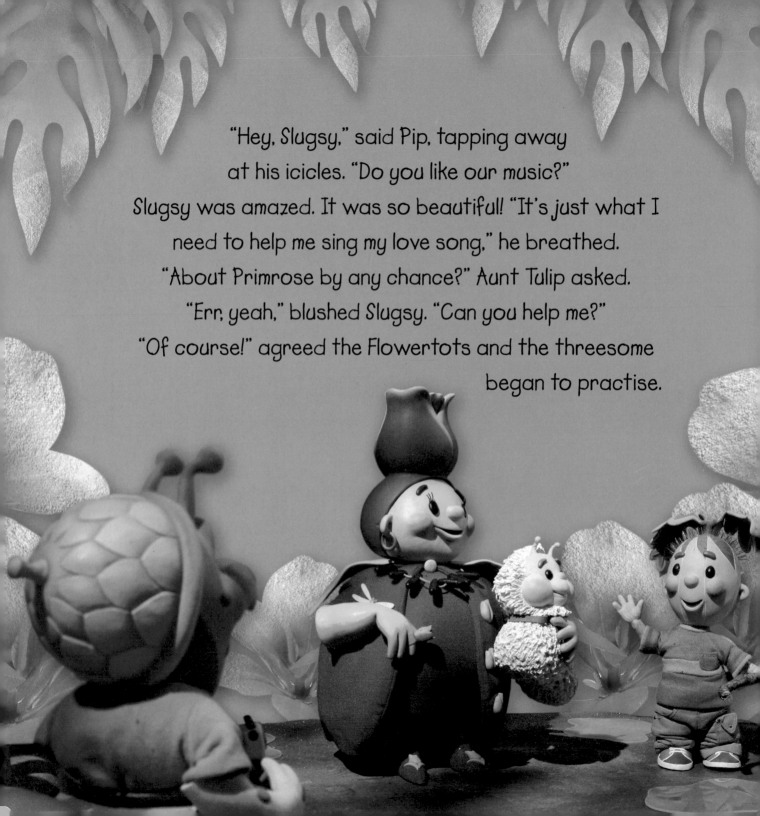

"Hey, Slugsy," said Pip, tapping away
at his icicles. "Do you like our music?"
Slugsy was amazed. It was so beautiful! "It's just what I
need to help me sing my love song," he breathed.
"About Primrose by any chance?" Aunt Tulip asked.
"Err, yeah," blushed Slugsy. "Can you help me?"
"Of course!" agreed the Flowertots and the threesome
began to practise.

"Our pipes are frozen. Can we borrow
some water?" Primrose asked.
"Oh dear," said Fifi, "my pipes are frozen up too.
Unless Stingo has managed to fix them
yet?" All the Tots turned to look
at Stingo, who was snoring
loudly at the table.
"I knew it!"
said Bumble, testing the taps.
"He's eaten all the toast
and done nothing!"

"Get on the job you lazy wasp, or I'll..."
Primrose threatened. Stingo woke with
a start and quickly buzzed under the sink.
"What do I do?" he panicked.
Just as Stingo began tinkering
with his tools, the Flowertots
heard Pip's icicle music
accompanying Slugsy's
singing outside the cottage.
"What's that?"
Primrose wondered as she
heard her name in the song.

In the cold, frosty garden, Slugsy sang his song to Primrose.

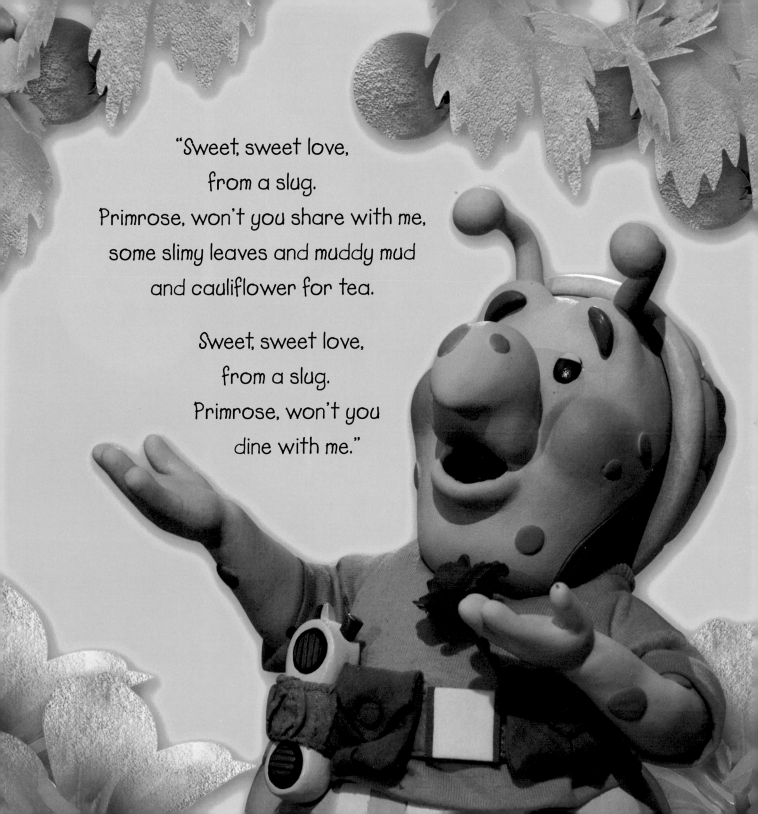

"Sweet, sweet love,
from a slug.
Primrose, won't you share with me,
some slimy leaves and muddy mud
and cauliflower for tea.

Sweet, sweet love,
from a slug.
Primrose, won't you
dine with me."

"Er, that was very sweet, Slugsy"
blushed Primrose.
"Ssso will you ssshare my sssupper
with me tonight?"asked Slugsy.
"OK," smiled Primrose kindly.
"OK, as in OK? Ssslimy Ssslug Trailsss!"
Slugsy was very happy.

"I don't know how any of us will cook
dinner with the pipes all frozen."
Fifi sighed. Just then, the
sun peeped out from
behind a cloud.
"Bouncing Buttercups,
the sun's come out!"
laughed Bumble.
And slowly but surely, the
sun began to melt all the ice.

Stingo was still boasting
when Bumble appeared with
a fresh plate of honey toast.
"As I was saying, as a top
class handyman, I can handle
any job in return for-"
"A slice of honey toast?"
Before Stingo could finish his
sentence, Fifi filled his mouth
with a giant, buttery slice!
"Mmmmm!"
agreed Stingo as all
the Flowertots laughed.

Make Your Own Honey Toast

This recipe is very easy to make but you will need a grown-up to help you too. Oooh, I can almost taste that toast!

Toast

You will need:

6 slices white bread

3 medium eggs - slightly beaten

1/4 cup milk

3 Tablespoons honey

1/8 teaspoon nutmeg

1. Whisk eggs with milk, honey and nutmeg in a small bowl until they are smooth and runny.

2. Now pour your eggy-honey mixture over bread and let it soak in for a couple minutes until it's soft.

3. Now ask your grown up helper to brown both sides of each slice of bread on hot greased griddle pan.
It should only need about 2 minutes each side.

* ALWAYS GET A GROWN - UP TO HELP IN THE KITCHEN!

Fifi and the Flowertots

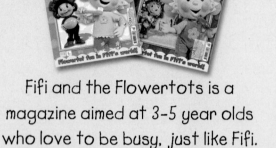

Talking Fifi
Forget-Me-Not

Fifi and the Flowertots is a magazine aimed at 3-5 year olds who love to be busy, just like Fifi. Join the Flowertot fun in Fifi's world!

Push 'n' Go Mo

Talk 'n'
Sneeze
Bumble

Have even more Flowertot fun with these Fifi story and activity books!

Chocolate
Surprise
is out
on DVD
now!

Forget-Me-Not
Cottage Playset

Visit Fifi at www.fifiandtheflowertots.com